Abracadabra Violin Repertoire

Violin Part

Contents

Moscow nights	2
Over the rainbow	3
The singing bird	4
All through the night	4
We said we wouldn't look back	5
Mighty like a rose	6
Tambourin (Rameau)	6
Blow the wind southerly	7
Plaisir d'amour	7
Ascot gavotte	8
Theme from The Bridges of Paris	9
The golden peacock	10
When you wish upon a star	10
The water is wide	11
Minuet (Boccherini)	12
Three train travel tunes:	
1 Off we go!	12
2 Scene through the window	14
3 Full speed ahead!	15

A & C Black · London

Moscow nights

V Soloviev-Sedoy

Mighty like a rose

Ethelbert Nevin

Tambourin

melody by Rameau

The golden peacock

Jewish folk song

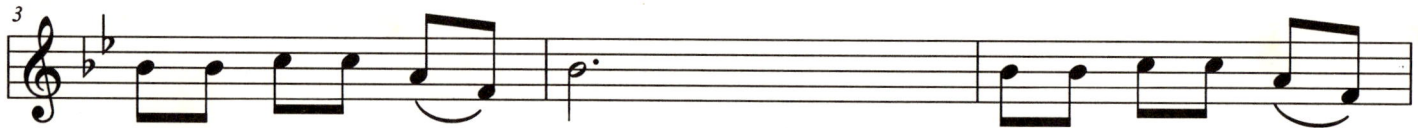

When you wish upon a star

Leigh Harline

The water is wide

traditional

Minuet

Boccherini (from Quintet No 5, Op 13)

Three train travel tunes

Michael Illman

1 Off we go!

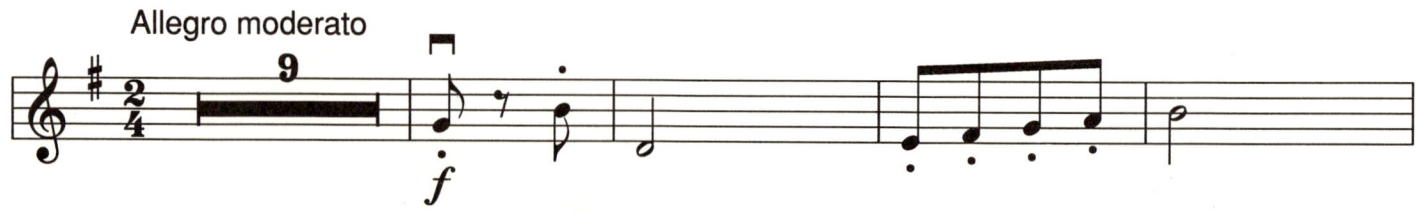

3 Full speed ahead!

Michael Illman

First published 1990 by A & C Black (Publishers) Ltd, 35 Bedford Row, London WC1R 4JH. © 1990 A & C Black (Publishers) Ltd.

ISBN 0-7136-3241-0

PHOTOCOPYING PROHIBITED. All rights reserved. No part of this publication may be reproduced, stored in a retrieval system or transmitted in any form or by any means, nor may it be photocopied or otherwise reproduced within the terms of any blanket licence scheme.

Acknowledgements

The publishers would like to thank the following, who have kindly granted permission for the reprinting of music:

Peter Davey for *Theme from The Bridges of Paris*

Michael Illman for *Three train travel tunes*

Chappell Music and International Music Publications for *Ascot Gavotte*: © 1956 Alan Jay Lerner and Frederick Loewe. Chappell & Co Inc USA. Reproduced by permission of Chappell Music Ltd and International Music Publications; and *When you wish upon a star*: © 1940 Bourne Inc USA. Reproduced by permission of Chappell Music Ltd and International Music Publications.

CPP/Belwin Inc and International Music Publications for *Over the Rainbow*: © 1938 & 1939 (renewed 1966 & 1967) Metro-Goldwyn-Meyer Inc USA. Reproduced by permission of CPP/Belwin Inc and International Music Publications.

EMI Music Publishing Ltd and International Music Publications for *We said we wouldn't look back*: © 1954 Francis Day and Hunter Ltd, London WC2 0EA. Reproduced by permission of EMI Music Publishing Ltd and International Music Publications.

Every effort has been made to trace and acknowledge copyright owners. If any right has been omitted the publishers offer their apologies and will seek to rectify this in subsequent editions.

Abracadabra Violin Repertoire

Piano Part

Contents

Moscow nights	2
Over the rainbow	4
The singing bird	6
All through the night	7
We said we wouldn't look back	8
Mighty like a rose	10
Tambourin (Rameau)	11
Blow the wind southerly	12
Plaisir d'amour	13
Ascot gavotte	14
Theme from The Bridges of Paris	16
The golden peacock	19
When you wish upon a star	20
The water is wide	22
Minuet (Boccherini)	22
Three train travel tunes:	
1 Off we go!	24
2 Scene through the window	27
3 Full speed ahead!	30

A & C Black · London

Moscow nights

V Soloviev-Sedoy

Over the rainbow

Harold Arlen

The singing bird

folk song

All through the night

Welsh

We said we wouldn't look back

Julian Slade

Mighty like a rose

Ethelbert Nevin

Tambourin

melody by Rameau

Blow the wind southerly

folk song

Plaisir d'amour

G P Martini

Ascot gavotte

Lerner and Loewe

Theme from The Bridges of Paris

Peter Davey

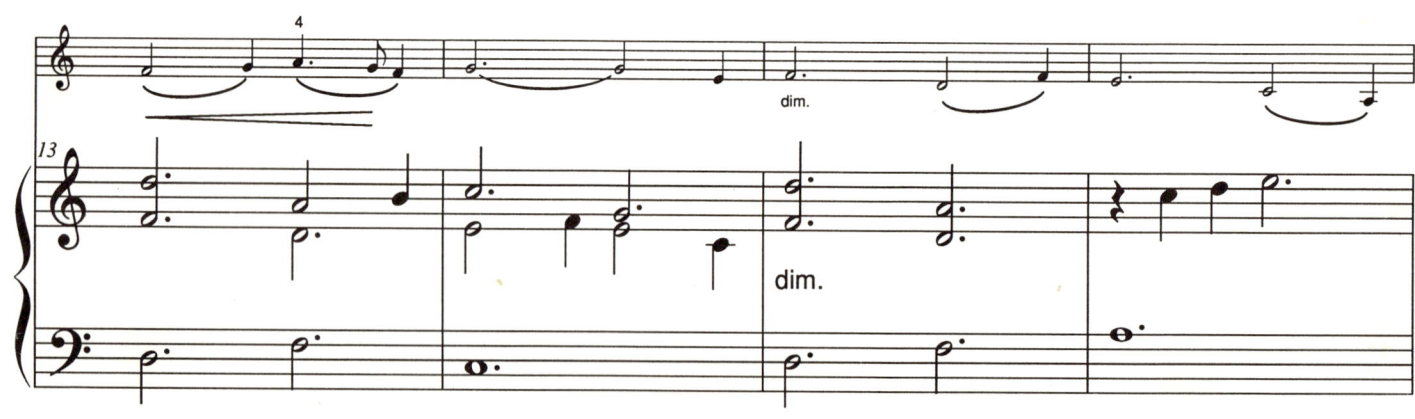

turn over

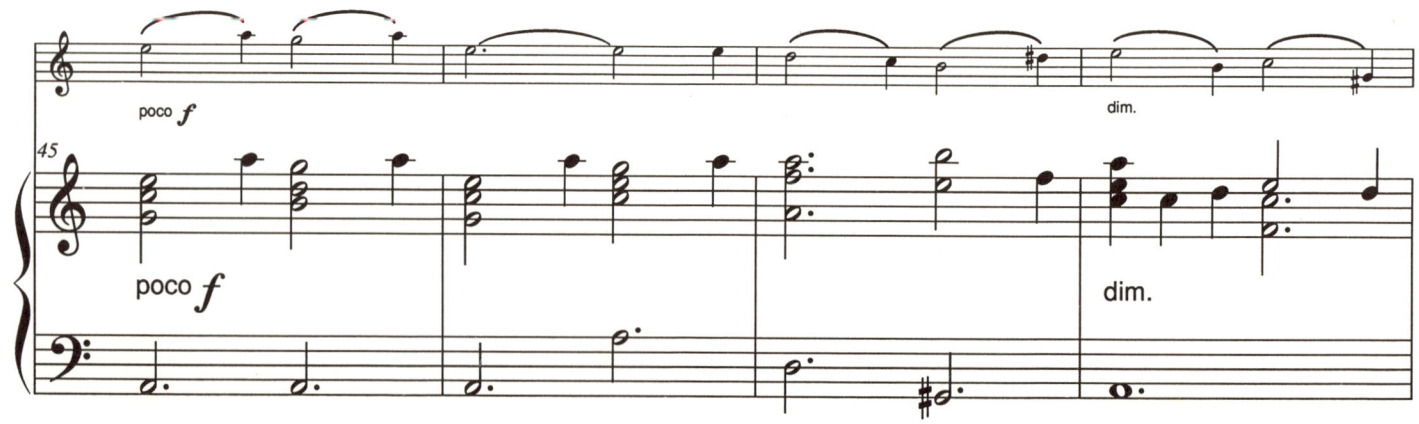

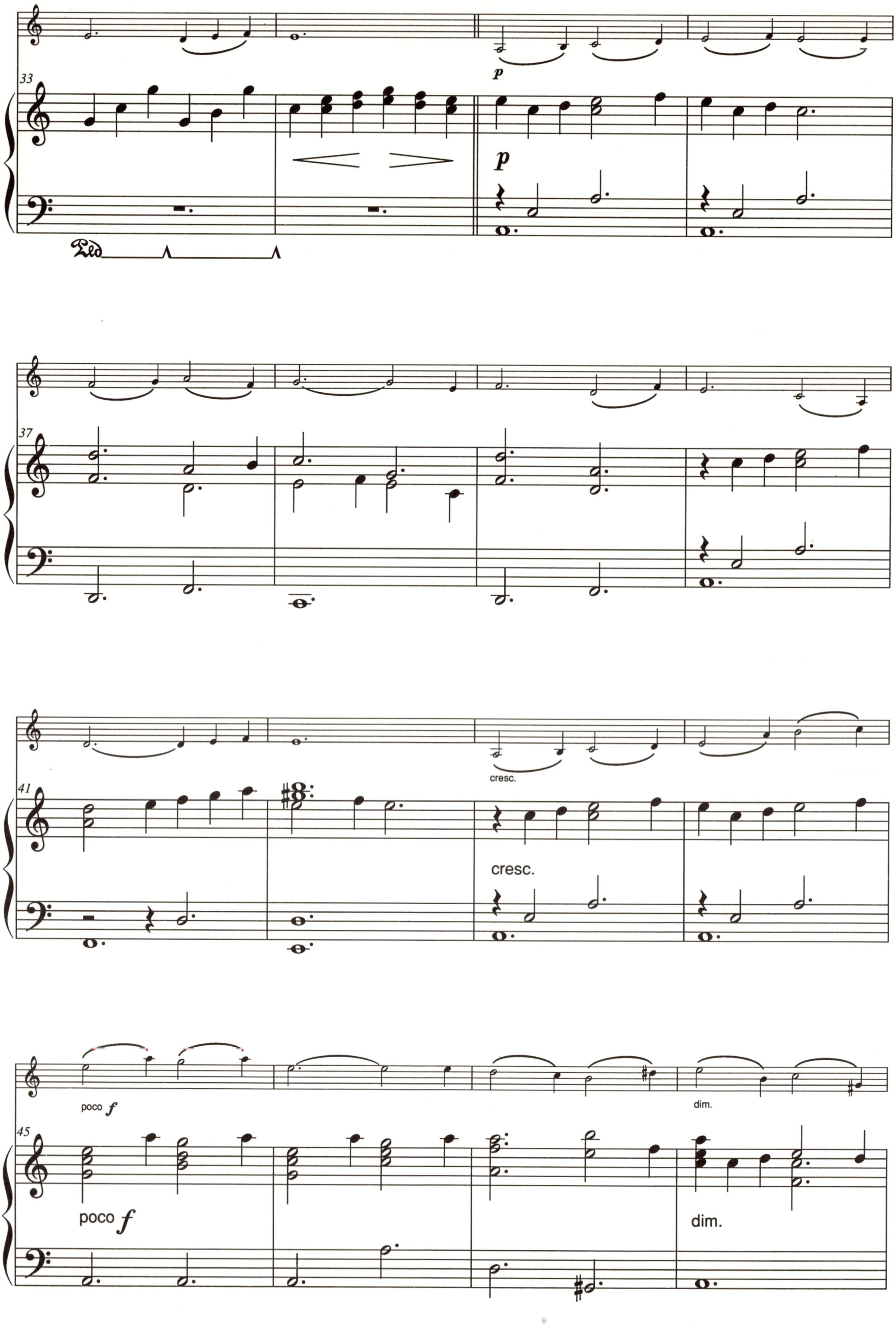
33
p
p
37
41
cresc.
cresc.
45
poco f
poco f
dim.
dim.

The golden peacock

Jewish folk song

When you wish upon a star

Leigh Harline

21

The water is wide

traditional

Slowly

Minuet

Boccherini (from Quintet No 5, Op 13)

Andante grazioso

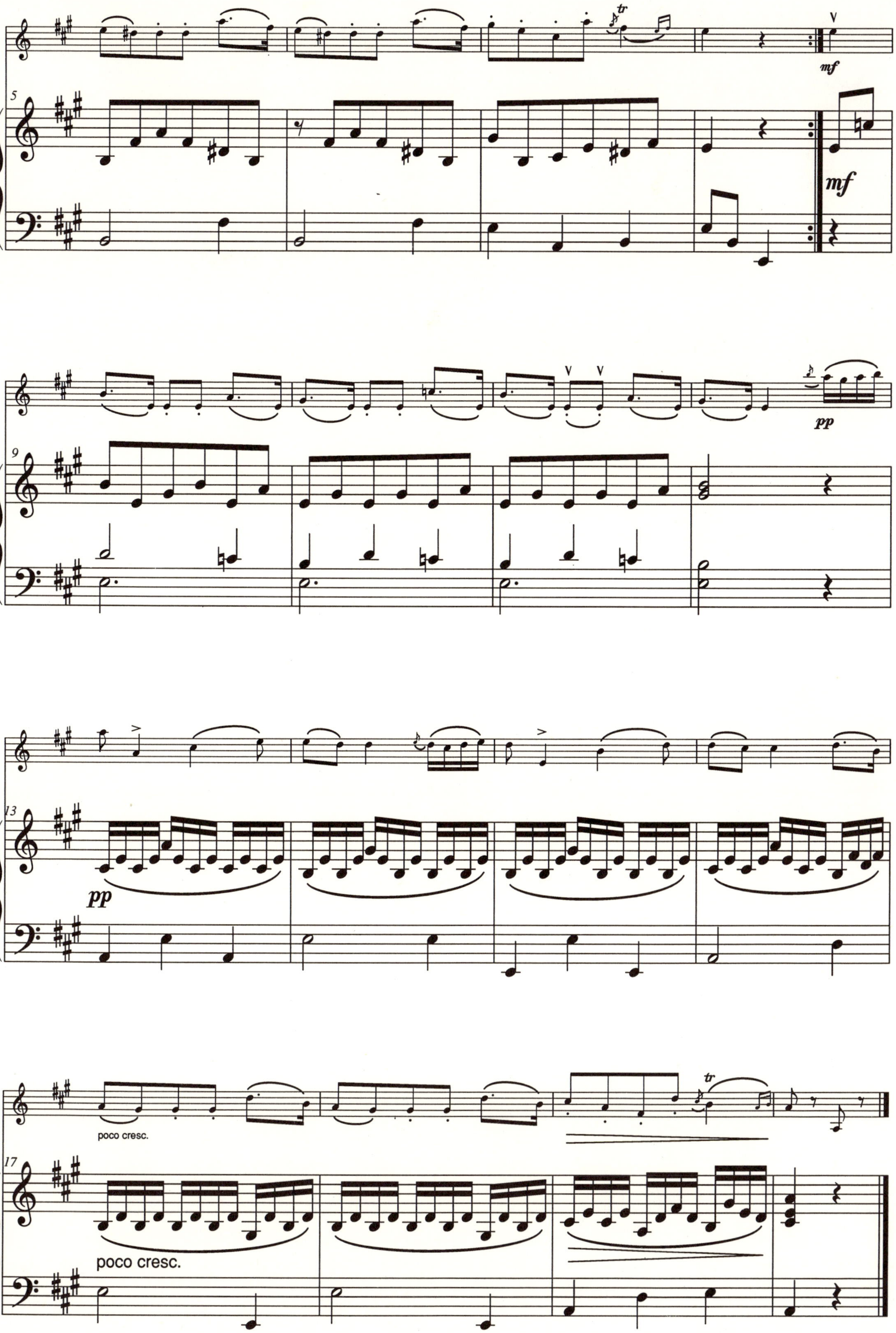
5
tr
mf
mf
9
pp
13
pp
17
poco cresc.
poco cresc.
tr

Three train travel tunes

1 Off we go!

Michael Illman

Allegro moderato

sempre staccato

25

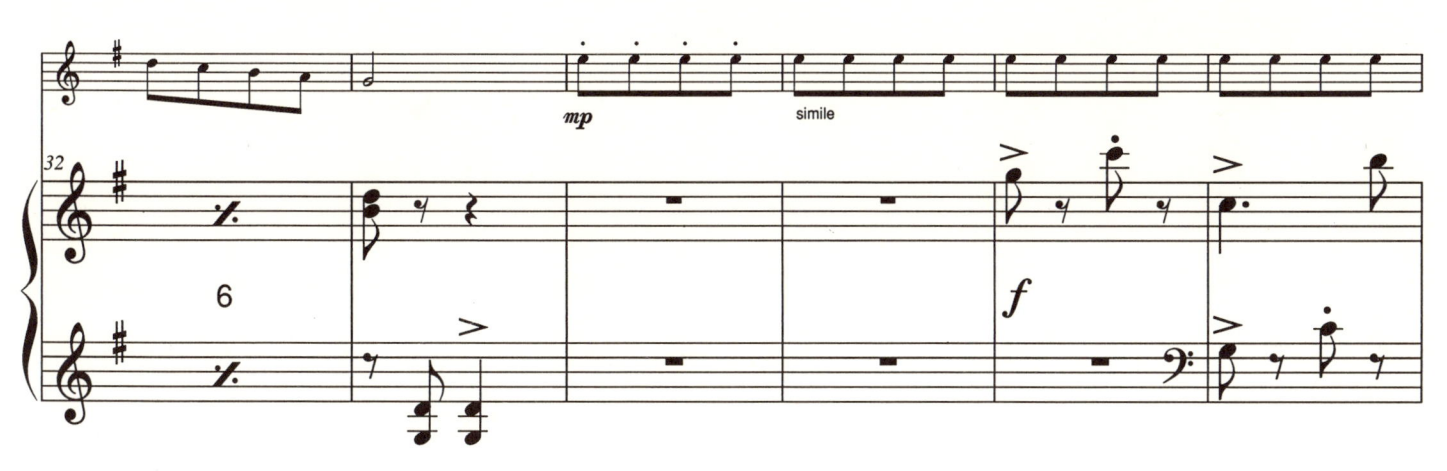

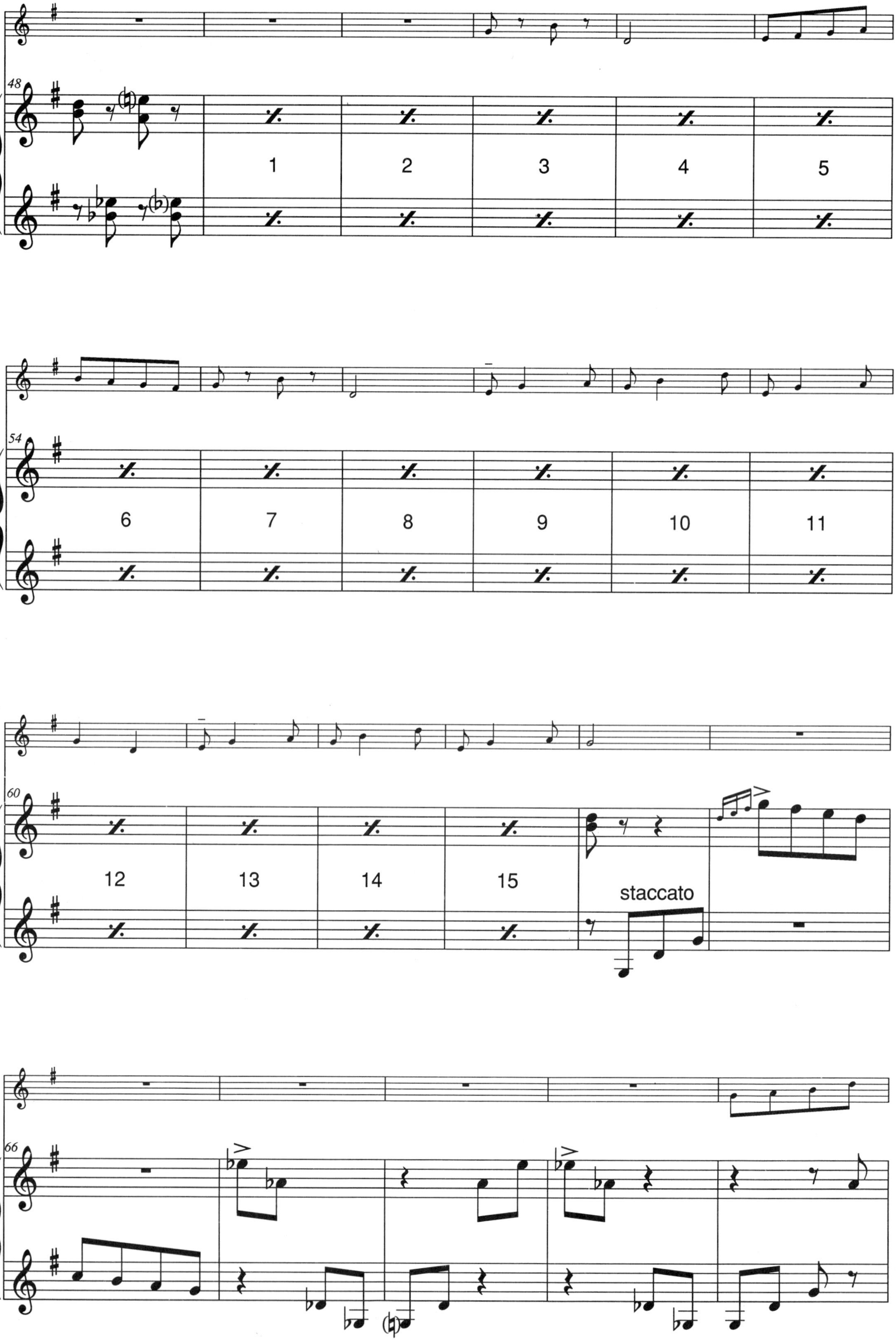
48
1
2
3
4
5
54
6
7
8
9
10
11
60
12
13
14
15
staccato
66

2 Scene through the window

Michael Illman

Andante con moto

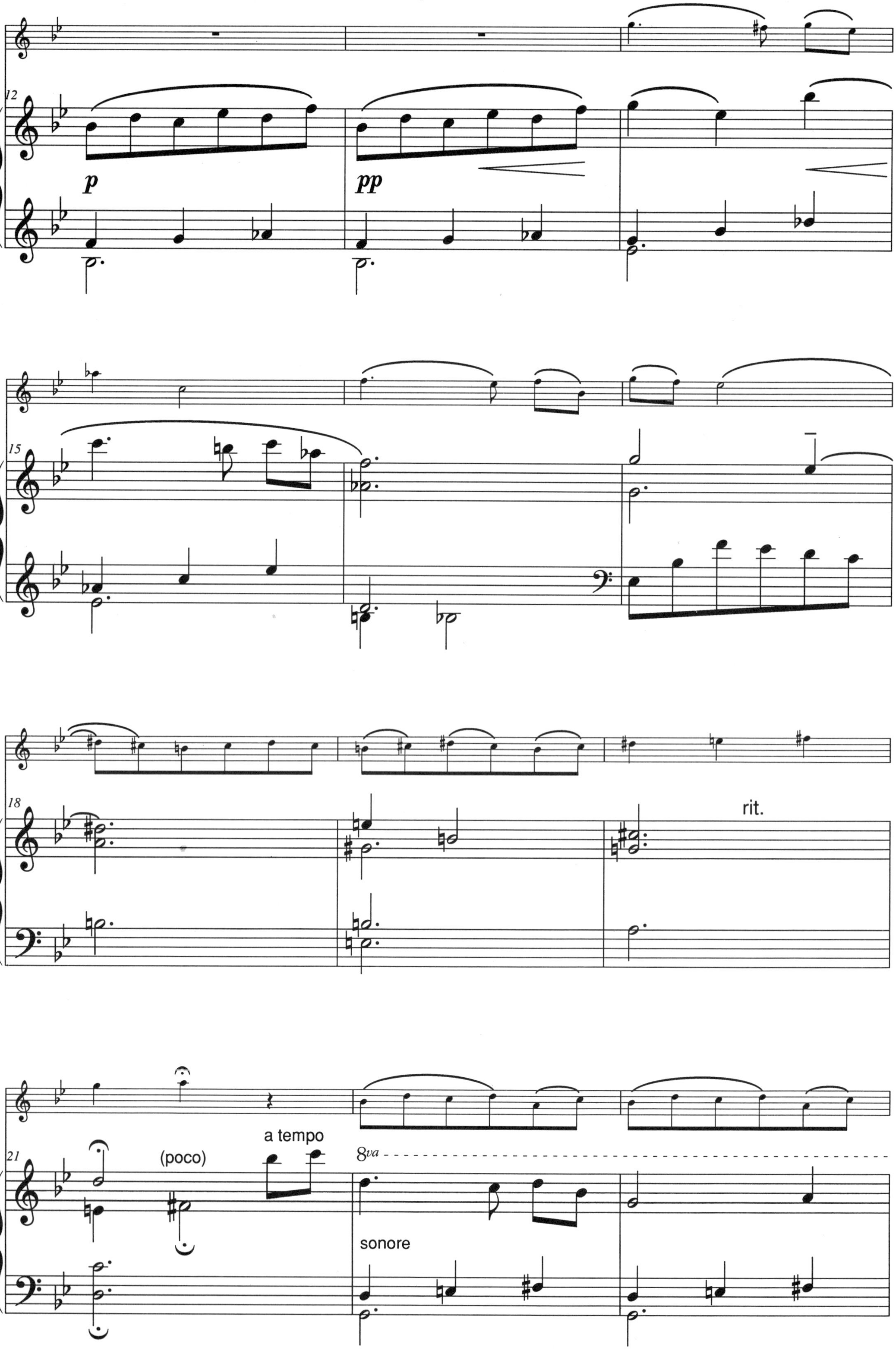
12
p
pp
15
18
rit.
21
(poco)
a tempo
8va
sonore

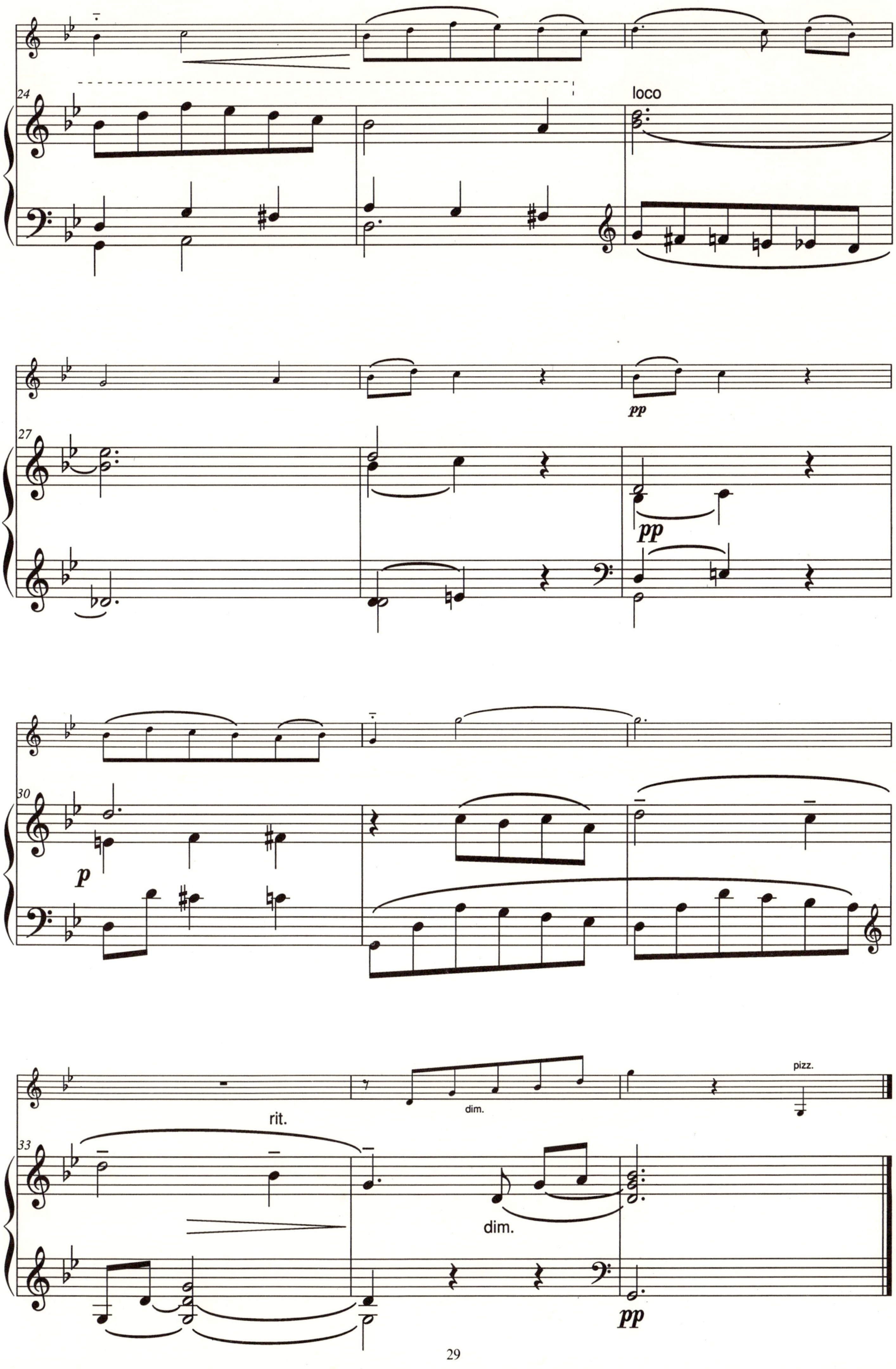
24
loco
27
pp
pp
30
p
rit.
33
dim.
dim.
pizz.
pp

3 Full speed ahead!

Michael Illman

articulato

rit.
rit. e dim.
Turn over

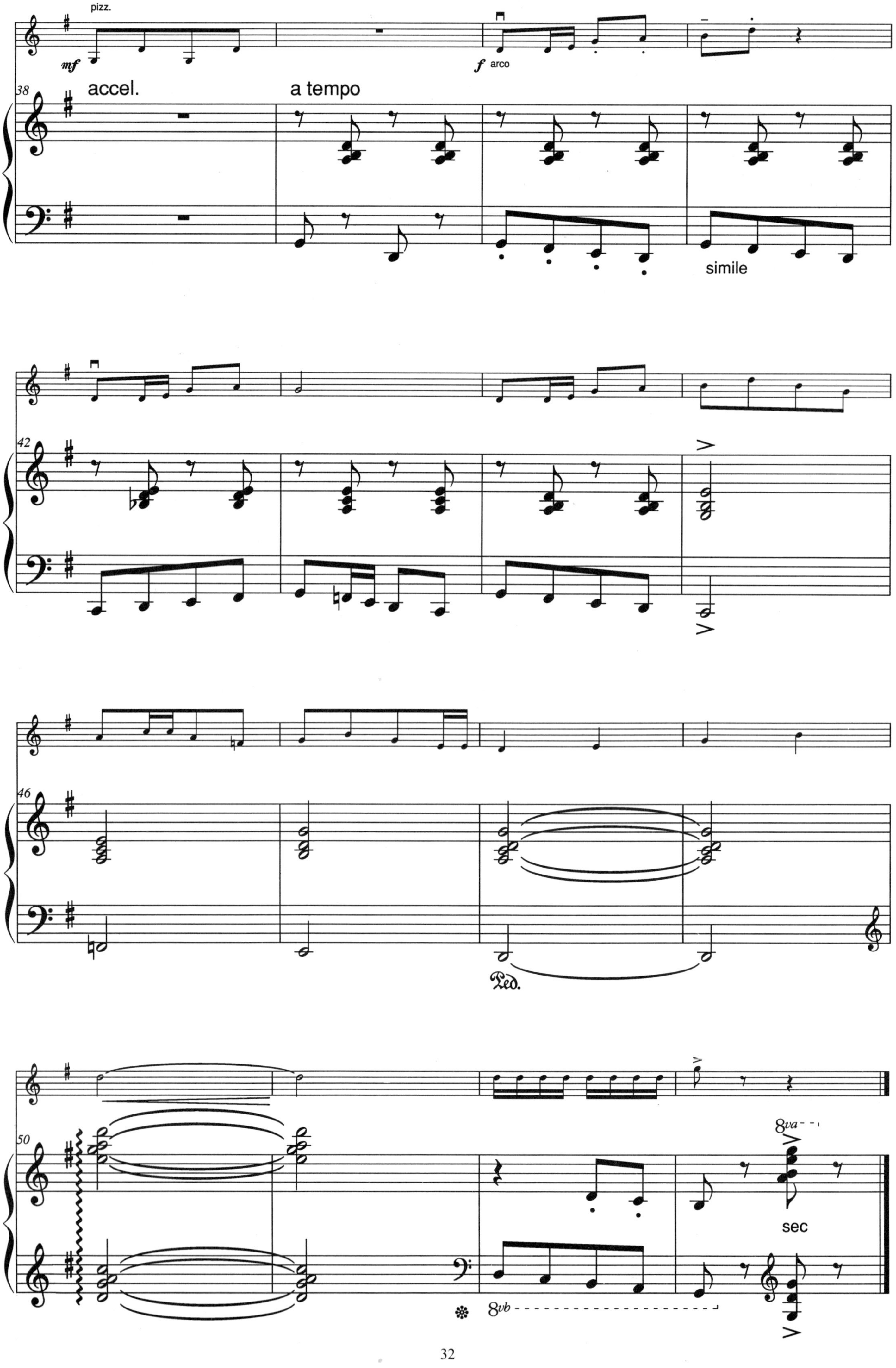
pizz.
mf
f arco
38
accel.
a tempo
simile
42
46
Ped.
50
8va
sec
8vb